The Practical Princess

by JAY WILLIAMS   *pictures by* FRISO HENSTRA

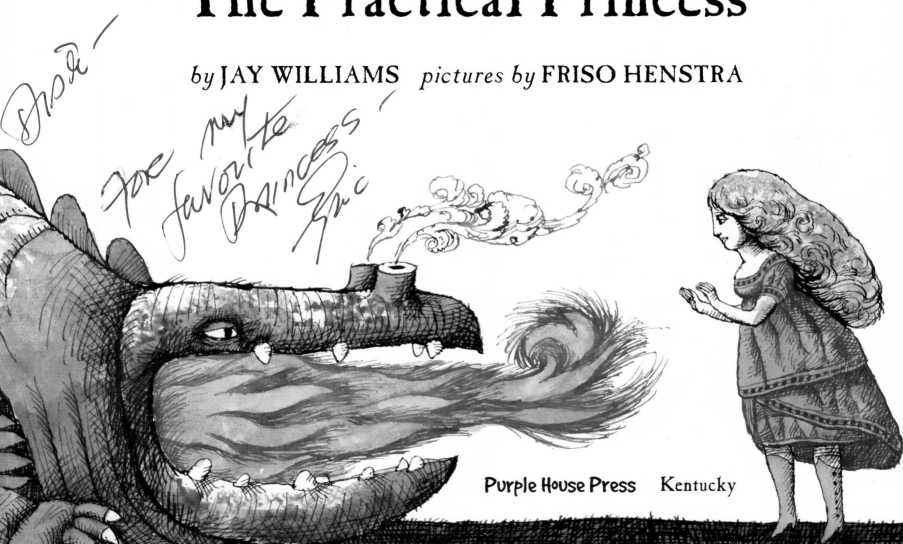

Purple House Press   Kentucky

Published by
Purple House Press
PO Box 787, Cynthiana, Kentucky 41031

Text copyright © 1969 by Jay Williams. Copyright © renewed 1997.
Illustrations copyright © 1969 by Friso Henstra. Copyright © renewed 1997.
Published by arrangement with Aladdin, an imprint of Simon & Schuster
Children's Publishing Division.

Summary: A princess uses common sense to get rid of a dragon, save herself from imprisonment, and find a handsome prince.

ISBN13: 978-1-930900-90-5   LCCN: 2016943773

Find more Classic Books for Kids at
purplehousepress.com

Printed in South Korea by PACOM
1 2 3 4 5 6 7 8 9 10
First Edition

This book is for my grandson, Ben.

Princess Bedelia was as lovely as the moon shining upon a lake full of waterlilies. She was as graceful as a cat leaping. And she was also extremely practical.

When she was born, three fairies had come to her cradle to give her gifts as was usual in that country. The first fairy had given her beauty. The second had given her grace. But the third, who was a wise old creature, had said, "I give her common sense."

"I don't think much of that gift," said King Ludwig, raising his eyebrows. "What good is common sense to a princess? All she needs is charm."

Nevertheless, when Bedelia was eighteen years old, something happened which made the king change his mind.

A dragon moved into the neighborhood. He settled in a dark cave on top of a mountain, and the first thing he did was to send a message to the king. "I must have a princess to devour," the message said, "or I shall breathe out my fiery breath and destroy the kingdom."

Sadly, King Ludwig called together his councillors and read them the message.
"Perhaps," said the Prime Minister, "we had better advertise for a knight to slay the dragon. That is what is generally done in these cases."
"I'm afraid we haven't time," answered the king. "The dragon has only given us until tomorrow morning. There is no help for it. We shall have to send him the princess."
Princess Bedelia had come to the meeting because, as she said, she liked to mind her own business and this was certainly her business.
"Rubbish!" she said. "Dragons can't tell the difference between princesses and anyone else. Use your common sense. He's just asking for me because he's a snob."

"That may be so," said her father, "but if we don't send you along, he'll destroy the kingdom."

"Right!" said Bedelia. "I see I'll have to deal with this myself." She left the council chamber. She got the largest and gaudiest of her state robes and stuffed it with straw, and tied it together with string. Into the center of the bundle she packed about a hundred pounds of gunpowder. She got two strong young men to carry it up the mountain for her. She stood in front of the dragon's cave and called, "Come out! Here's the princess!" The dragon came blinking and peering out of the darkness. Seeing the bright robe covered with gold and silver embroidery, and hearing Bedelia's voice, he opened his mouth wide.

At once, at Bedelia's signal, the two young men swung the robe and gave it a good heave, right down the dragon's throat. Bedelia threw herself flat on the ground, and the two young men ran.

As the gunpowder met the flames inside the dragon, there was a tremendous explosion.

Bedelia got up, dusting herself off. "Dragons," she said, "are not very bright."

She left the two young men sweeping up the pieces, and she went back to the castle to have her geography lesson.

The lesson that morning was local geography. "Our kingdom, Arapathia, is bounded on the north by Istven," said the teacher. "Lord Garp, the ruler of Istven, is old, crafty, rich, and greedy."

At that very moment, Lord Garp of Istven was arriving at the castle. Word of Bedelia's destruction of the dragon had reached him. "The girl," said he, "is just the wife for me." And he had come with a hundred finely-dressed courtiers and many presents to ask King Ludwig for her hand.

The king sent for Bedelia. "My dear," he said, clearing his throat nervously, "just see who is here."

"I see. It's Lord Garp," said Bedelia. She turned to go.

"He wants to marry you," said the king.

Bedelia looked at Lord Garp. His face was like an old napkin, crumpled and wrinkled. It was covered with warts, as if someone had left crumbs on the napkin. He had only two teeth. Six long hairs grew from his chin, and none on his head. She felt like screaming.

However, she said, "I'm very flattered. Thank you, Lord Garp. Just let me talk to my father in private for a minute." When they had retired to a small room behind the throne, Bedelia said to the king, "What will Lord Garp do if I refuse to marry him?"

"He is rich, greedy, and crafty," said the king, unhappily. "He is also used to having his own way in everything. He will be insulted. He will probably declare war on us, and then there will be trouble."

"Very well," said Bedelia. "We must be practical."

She returned to the throne room. Smiling sweetly at Lord Garp, she said, "My lord, as you know, it is customary for a princess to set tasks for anyone who wishes to marry her. Surely, you wouldn't like me to break the custom. And you are bold and powerful enough, I know, to perform any task."

"That is true," said Lord Garp, smugly, stroking the six hairs on his chin. "Name your task."

"Bring me," said Bedelia, "a branch from the Jewel Tree of Paxis."

Lord Garp bowed, and off he went. "I think," said Bedelia to her father, "that we have seen the last of him. For Paxis is a thousand miles away, and the Jewel Tree is guarded by lions, serpents, and wolves."

But in two weeks, Lord Garp was back. With him he bore a chest, and from the chest he took a wonderful twig. Its bark was of rough gold. The leaves that grew from it were of fine silver. The twig was covered with blossoms, and each blossom had petals of mother-of-pearl and centers of sapphires, the color of the evening sky.

Bedelia's heart sank as she took the twig. But then she said to herself, "Use your common sense, my girl! Lord Garp never traveled two thousand miles in two weeks, nor is he the man to fight his way through lions, serpents, and wolves."

She looked more carefully at the branch. Then she said, "My lord, you know that the Jewel Tree of Paxis is a living tree, although it is all made of jewels."

"Why, of course," said Lord Garp. "Everyone knows that."

"Well," said Bedelia, "then why is it that these blossoms have no scent?"

Lord Garp turned red.

"I think," Bedelia went on, "that this branch was made by the jewelers of Istven, who are the best in the world. Not very nice of you, my lord. Some people might even call it cheating." Lord Garp shrugged. He was too old and rich to feel ashamed. But like many men used to having their own way, the more Bedelia refused him, the more he was determined to have her. "Never mind all that," he said. "Set me another task. This time, I swear I will perform it."

Bedelia sighed. "Very well. Then bring me a cloak made from the skins of the salamanders who live in the Volcano of Scoria."

Lord Garp bowed, and off he went. "The Volcano of Scoria," said Bedelia to her father, "is covered with red-hot lava. It burns steadily with great flames, and pours out poisonous smoke so that no one can come within a mile of it."

"You have certainly profited by your geography lessons," said the king, with admiration.

Nevertheless, in a week, Lord Garp was back. This time, he carried a cloak that shone and rippled with all the colors of fire. It was made of scaly skins, stitched together with fine golden wire. Each scale was red and orange and blue, like a tiny flame. Bedelia took the splendid cloak. She said to herself, "Use your head, miss! Lord Garp never climbed the red-hot slopes of the Volcano of Scoria."

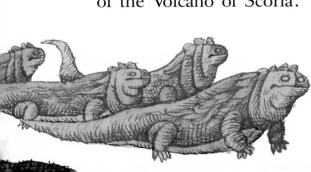

A fire was burning in the fireplace of the throne room. Bedelia hurled the cloak into it. The skins blazed up in a flash, blackened, and fell to ashes.

Lord Garp's mouth fell open. Before he could speak, Bedelia said, "That cloak was a fake, my lord. The skins of salamanders who can live in the Volcano of Scoria wouldn't burn in a little fire like that one."

Lord Garp turned pale with anger. He hopped up and down, unable at first to do anything but splutter.

"Ub—ub—ub!" he cried. Then, controlling himself, he said, "So be it. If I can't have you, no one shall!"

He pointed a long, skinny finger at her. On the finger was a magic ring. At once, a great wind arose. It blew through the throne room. It sent King Ludwig flying one way and his guards the other. Bedelia was picked up and whisked off through the air. When she could catch her breath and look about her, she found herself in a room at the top of a tower.

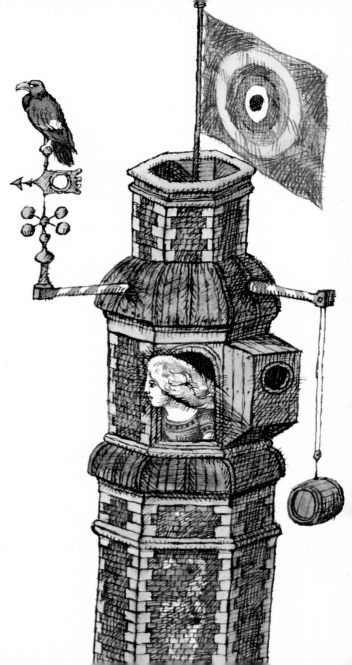

Bedelia peered out of the window. About the tower stretched an empty, barren plain. As she watched, a speck appeared in the distance. A plume of dust rose behind it. It drew nearer and became Lord Garp on horseback.

He rode to the tower and looked up at Bedelia. "Aha!" he croaked. "So you are safe and snug, are you? And will you marry me now?"

"Never," said Bedelia, firmly.

"Then stay there until never comes," snarled Lord Garp. Away he rode.

For the next two days, Bedelia felt very sorry for herself. She sat wistfully by the window, looking out at the empty plain. When she was hungry, food appeared on the table. When she was tired, she lay down on the narrow cot and slept. Each day, Lord Garp rode by and asked if she had changed her mind, and each day she refused him. Her only hope was that, as so often happens in old tales, a prince might come riding by who would rescue her.

But on the third day, she gave herself a shake.

"Now, then, pull yourself together," she said, sternly. "If you sit waiting for a prince to rescue you, you may sit here forever. Be practical! If there's any rescuing to be done, you're going to have to do it yourself."

She jumped up. There was something she had not yet done, and now she did it. She tried the door.

It opened.

Outside, were three other doors. But there was no sign of a stair, or any way down from the top of the tower.

She opened two of the doors and found that they led into cells just like hers, but empty. Behind the fourth door, however, lay what appeared to be a haystack.

From beneath it came the sound of snores. And between snores, a voice said, "Six million and twelve...*snore*...six million and thirteen...*snore*...six million and fourteen..."

Cautiously, she went closer. Then she saw that what she had taken for a haystack was in fact an immense pile of blond hair. Parting it, she found a young man, sound asleep.

As she stared, he opened his eyes. He blinked at her. "Who—?" he said. Then he said, "Six million and fifteen," closed his eyes, and fell asleep again.

Bedelia took him by the shoulder and shook him hard. He awoke, yawning, and tried to sit up. But the mass of hair made this difficult.

"What on earth is the matter with you?" Bedelia asked. "Who are you?"

"I am Prince Perian," he replied, "the rightful ruler of—oh, dear, here I go again. Six million and…" His eyes began to close.

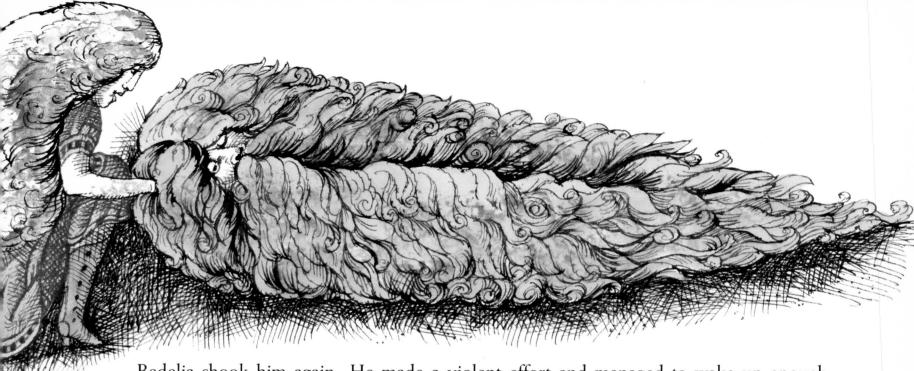

Bedelia shook him again. He made a violent effort and managed to wake up enough to continue, "—of Istven. But Lord Garp has put me under a spell. I have to count sheep jumping over a fence, and this puts me to slee—ee—ee—"
He began to snore lightly.
"Dear me," said Bedelia. "I must do something."
She thought hard. Then she pinched Perian's ear, and this woke him with a start.
"Listen," she said. "It's quite simple. It's all in your mind, you see. You are imagining the sheep jumping over the fence—No! Don't go to sleep again!

"This is what you must do. Imagine them jumping backwards. As you do, *count* them backwards, and when you get to *one*, you'll be wide awake."

The prince's eyes snapped open. "Marvelous!" he said. "Will it work?"

"It's bound to," said Bedelia. "If the sheep going one way will put you to sleep, their going back again will wake you up."

Hastily, the prince began to count, "Six million and fourteen, six million and thirteen, six million and twelve..."

"Oh, my goodness," cried Bedelia, "count by hundreds, or you'll never get there."

He began to gabble as fast as he could, and with each moment that passed, his eyes sparkled more brightly, his face grew livelier, and he seemed a little stronger, until at last he shouted, "Five, four, three, two, ONE!" and awoke completely.

He struggled to his feet, with a little help from Bedelia.

"Heavens!" he said. "Look how my hair and beard have grown. I've been here for years. Thank you, my dear. Who are you, and what are you doing here?"

Bedelia quickly explained.

Perian shook his head. "One more crime of Lord Garp's," he said. "We must escape and see that he is punished."

"Easier said than done," Bedelia replied. "There is no stair in this tower, as far as I can tell, and the outside wall is much too smooth to climb down."

Perian frowned. "This will take some thought," he said. "What we need is a long rope."

"Use your common sense," said Bedelia. "We haven't any rope."

Then her face lighted, and she clapped her hands. "But we have your beard," she laughed.

Perian understood at once, and chuckled. "I'm sure it will reach almost to the ground," he said. "But we haven't any scissors to cut it off with."

"That is so," said Bedelia. "Hang it out of the window and let me climb down. I'll search the tower and perhaps I can find a ladder, or a hidden stair. If all else fails, I can go for help."

She and the prince gathered up great armfuls of the beard and staggered into Bedelia's room, which had the largest window. The prince's long hair trailed behind and nearly tripped him.

Perian threw the beard out of the window and braced himself, holding the beard with both hands to ease the pull on his chin. Bedelia climbed out of the window and slid down the beard.

But suddenly, out of the wilderness came the drumming of hoofs, a cloud of dust, and then Lord Garp on his swift horse.

With once glance, he saw what was happening. He shook his fist up at Prince Perian.

"Meddlesome fool!" he shouted. "I'll teach you to interfere." He leaped from the horse and grabbed the beard. He gave it a tremendous yank. Headfirst came Perian, out of the window. Down he fell, and with a thump, he landed right on top of old Lord Garp.

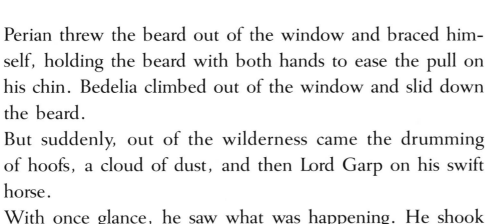
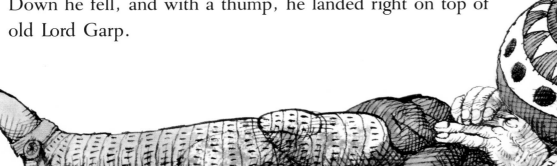

This saved Perian, who was not hurt at all. But it was the end of Lord Garp.

Perian and Bedelia rode back to Istven on Lord Garp's horse. In the great city, the prince was greeted with cheers of joy— once everyone had recognized him after so many years and under so much hair.

And of course, since Bedelia had rescued him from captivity, she married him. First, however, she made him get a haircut and a shave so that she could see what he really looked like. For she was always practical.

King Ludwig

The Dragon

ARAPATHIA

LudwigTown

Bedelia

Jewel Tree

Lord Garp

ISTVEN

PAXIS

Prince Perian

Istven City

Volcano of Scoria

N